FROGGY'S BEST CHRISTMAS

FROGGY'S BEST CHRISTMAS

by JONATHAN LONDON
illustrated by FRANK REMKIEWICZ

SCHOLASTIC INC.
New York Toronto London Auckland Sydney
Mexico City New Delhi Hong Kong Buenos Aires

For Valerie and Monica Lewis—with their love of books for children,
and for Walter "the Giant Storyteller" Mayes
    —J. L.

For Grace Nissley, Merry Christmas
    —F. R.

ISBN 0-439-31442-9

12 11 10 9 8 7 6 5   2 3 4 5 6/0

Printed in the U.S.A.   08

First Scholastic printing, November 2001

Set in Kabel

It was the night before Christmas
and Froggy was dreaming of snow.
He had months of dreaming to go
before it was time to wake up
for spring.

Thump! thump!
In the dream, Max was tossing snowballs
against Froggy's window.

FRROOGGYY !

called his friend.
"Wha-a-a-t?"
But it wasn't a dream at all.
Froggy woke up
and looked out the window.
"Max! Max!" he shouted.

He hopped out of bed—*flop flop flop*—
and opened the door.
"MERRY CHRISTMAS, FROGGY!" yelled Max
and gave him a present.

"Wow!" said Froggy. "This is my *first* Christmas present!"
"This is your first *Christmas*!" said Max. "You always sleep through it!"
"I've heard all about Christmas," said Froggy. "Now I can celebrate it! Yippee!"
And Froggy went to look for a gift for Max—*flop flop flop*.

"I found the perfect one!" he said.
"What is it?" asked Max as he tore open the box.
"My soccer ball—the one I kicked
for our winning goal at City Cup!"
"Gee, thanks," said Max,
juggling the ball
on his knees. "Now open
your present."

Froggy tore off the wrapping paper and opened the box.
Inside, there was a drawing of a Christmas tree.
"Gee, thanks," said Froggy. "I always wanted a drawing
of a Christmas tree."

"No, no!" said Max. "I'm giving you
a *real* Christmas tree!"
"Wow!" said Froggy. "What a friend!"
"Christmas," Max said, "is about friends."
"Yes!" shouted Froggy.
"Let's go find Matthew and Travis!"

And he rushed to his room
to get dressed—*zoop! Zip! Zut zut zut!*
Zup! Znap! Zat! Zwit! Zum!
Then he flopped outside—*flop flop flop.*

FRROOGGYY!

called Max
"Wha-a-a-t?"
"Did you forget something?"
"What?"
"Me!" And together they went off through the snow
to wake up their friends from their long winter naps.

First, they woke up Matthew.
"Wake up, wake up!" they shouted.
And Matthew the Turtle yawned and crawled out
from his home beside the pond.

Then they woke up Travis.
"Wake up, wake up!" they shouted.
And Travis the Bear yawned
and crawled out from his cave
under the snow.

"Merry Christmas! Merry Christmas!" said Froggy and Max.
"This is my first Christmas ever!" said Matthew.
"Mine, too!" said Travis.
And together they all trudged off through the snow
to find the perfect Christmas tree.

"Here's one!" cried Froggy
"Naw, it's too skinny," said Max.
"Here's one!" said Matthew.
"Naw, it's too fat," said Max.

"Here's one!" he hollered. "The perfect tree!"
And Max the Beaver gnawed . . . and gnawed . . .
and gnawed . . . until—

"Timber!"—*thunk!*
Then, together, they dragged the tree
home through the snow.

"Christmas," said Max when they got there, "is about friends . . .
and family, too."
And he scampered off and came back
with his grandma and grandpa.

And with everybody's help, Froggy put up the tree and trimmed it with popcorn chains and pinecones.

Then, with some paint and glue,
Froggy turned the biggest cone into a
tiny tree, and wrapped it for his dad . . .

painted and wrapped a picture for his mom . . .
and put them under the tree.

"It's not much," said Froggy,
"but Mom and Dad like it when
I make things all by myself."
"Besides," said Max, "it's the
spirit of giving
that counts."

"And *now*," said Froggy, "for the star!"

He made a star out of foil, then pushed a chair against the tree—
and climbed . . . and reached . . . and st-r-e-t-c-h-e-d . . .
"Timber!" shouted Max. *Thunk!*

FRROOGGYY!

yelled his mother and father.
"Wha-a-a-t?"
And in they came,
their eyes as big as sugarplums.

"Oops!" croaked Froggy,
looking more red in the face than green.
"Merry Christmas!"

And it *was* a merry Christmas!
Together they opened presents—*rrriiip!*

roasted chestnuts—*crrrackle!*

sang carols—"*Faaa lalaa la . . .*"

ate a feast—*munch crunch munch . . .*

and had a snowball fight—*oof!*

"This is my best Christmas ever," said Froggy.
"Ours, too!" said Matthew and Travis.
"This is your *first* Christmas ever!" said Max,
and everybody laughed.

"MERRY CHRISTMAS TO ALL!" shouted Froggy, and his friends waved good-bye.

"AND TO ALL A GOOD NIGHT!"
boomed Santa Owl.

HO HO HO!